Historically
Thinking

Historically
Thinking

MICHAEL HILLERY

HISTORICALLY THINKING

iUniverse books may be ordered through booksellers or by contacting:

iUniverse
1663 Liberty Drive
Bloomington, IN 47403
www.iuniverse.com
1-800-Authors (1-800-288-4677)

ISBN: 978-1-5320-4343-7 (sc)
ISBN: 978-1-5320-4344-4 (e)

Library of Congress Control Number: 2018902361

Print information available on the last page.

iUniverse rev. date: 03/06/2018

country. Is Quebec's identity jeopardized by including itself in the rest of Canada? Or is Quebec's nationhood separate from the rest of Canada? The question of identity and how history represents itself is a controversial one that applies to all societies. It needs to be examined.

The struggle for recognition of one's own culture under the power of a British umbrella government is especially apparent in the indigenous people's rights with the exclusion of their interests from public knowledge—and thus importance. Even the presentation of people of different cultures has been altered to suit the needs of this uniform vision of a nation. If you look at a film involving civilizations other than white Anglo-Saxon, the filmmakers often subject minorities to degradation out of habit or for the spectacle and the pursuit of making money. In the end, for what is history useful then? It is used not always to represent diverse cultures but to alienate people for a monetary purpose. John Dewey, an influential writer, believed that education was the foundation for any successful society and that through education a nation would become stronger by embedding in the youth the values of the people who wish to preserve their belief structure. Without some common link, passing from generation to generation, according to Dewey, how does one's society survive? The unification of history as a nation-building tool is exactly how some countries use the past to bring everyone together under one belief system. And once those countries come together under the same name, they then see themselves as greater than other nations around the world. This puts them in a position of needing colonies, much like the British Empire and the Americans in the Middle East. Once under one flag, they feel more powerful.

Before any external missions are under way, though, decisions from any government would embrace the importance of stability at home. That is where the use of history comes in, to bring everyone in the country together under one blanket of identity and then to try to establish that model for the rule of that government over its people in foreign lands. A country without a supporting population will have no influence upon other countries.

In the following pages, I explain the methods and practices that are used to affect societies here in Canada, in the United States and around the world, employing history as an essential part and thus emphasizing the importance of it.

On Historians

*B*EFORE ONE LOOKS at the impact that history has on the world stage, I would like to describe the significance it has within the boundaries of a country and how it is crucial to the survival of a society. In the Western world, for those who have a democratic government, history presents itself everywhere. It is taught in our schools as part of the official curriculum. And why does the government or the education department in these governments still put an emphasis on learning about the past? What purpose does it have, especially for the next generation of our people? And above all, what history should be taught to our students and in what way? Are other subjects more important in a technology-driven economy and job market? Finally, do we even need to learn history? Or should it lose its status as a subject and remain a conversation piece best suited for a small group of educators interested in the theory and not the practice of it?

When considering sources, both primary and secondary, there has always been a question as to their authenticity. Most primary sources are believed to have been empirical in the sense that they can be proven to be true; sometimes, they are even considered to be unbiased and untouched by any type of analytic thinker. Therefore, they have great value when building an argument because they cannot be disputed. Those types of sources up until recently have been books written by authors who simply recorded information, observations of natural phenomena, artifacts recovered from ancient sites in which they were found and original copies of newsprint or documentation, such as legal papers or logbooks. But recently, historians have examined oral evidence more closely. We have been accepting a wave of new pieces of our history into our grouping of primary sources, including drawings and traditional ceremonies. Oral history has long been seen as unreliable because of the unidentifiable nature of its physical substance. But through the transmission of those stories and traditions, we can gather an understanding of the past influence those words had, as they are reflective of past cultures, which can be studied today. Through word of mouth, historians can recover mounds of information about a civilization that has left behind no trace of written text.

The aboriginal histories come to mind as the best example of that type of transfer of history from generation to generation. Festivals and religious ceremonies recalled by elders give us a better view into the lives of the people who existed long before we arrived. The creation of the world story, which we all read in Canadian history books in school, barely scratches the surface of their lifestyles and traditions. These stories show an organized religion within each tribe, the status of members of their communities and their roles in economic, political and social life.

Before this proof became acceptable, another type of reliable source existed. These were Jesuit archives, recorded by religious men who explored deep into native territory. They made simple observations of the activities of those tribes, often painting them as savage and in need of Christianization. Would we not question the motives for what these Jesuits were recording if their only purpose rested in satisfying the needs of the church? It is those documents that have molded our view, as Canadians, of members of our society. Ceremonies, such as the potlatch and burial rituals, have organized structures governing them, which provide a culture of people who lived contrary to our beliefs. (The concept of sharing wealth upset many settlers, as greed for wealth was more important.) The ritual of burial and worship provided a religion that had its own congregation apart from Christianity, not to mention the evidence of organized civilizations well before the Europeans arrived. Could that have been the reason that oral histories have largely been ignored up until this point? Has the authenticity of primary sources been selected to suit the purpose of certain historians and not others?

The manipulation of resources, especially ones that are primary, is not new in the world in which we live. A great example of this concerns the controversy over the true identity of major figures in the past. Shakespeare, for example, has a long tradition of questions regarding who he actually was. The Stratfordian view offers the same and consistent thesis that he was a man from Stratford who mysteriously wrote all his plays and enjoyed great success; however, there have been many problems with that life story. Evidence points to various other explanations of who he was. Legal documents and common sense all suggest other explanations of the true identity of Shakespeare. This man who supposedly grew up poor had a prolific knowledge of Italy and events taking place around the world at the time. This information would not have been available for a poor boy in those days. Much like the assassination of John F. Kennedy, the accusations do fly about what really was happening behind the scenes. Nevertheless, one thing for sure was the resistance of scholars to admitting and disclosing information that might prove them wrong—or at least not right.

In order to do that, one would have to deny access to anyone who might uncover the truth and thus pose a threat to the established belief

3

History in the Media

*H*ISTORY HAS AN impact not only in the schools but also in the popular media as we know it today. There are a large number of films from around the world that are historically oriented. Not only do these reflect the lives of the people during that time, but they also contribute to the ever-changing discussion of history in our popular culture. Very often, historical films re-enact past moments that were benchmarks in the making of our understanding of long ago, for example, huge Hollywood blockbusters like *The Ten Commandments* and *Gone with the Wind*. Those types are often the high-budget films that cost a lot of money to produce because of the inclusion of popular actors, special effects, nice scenery and expensive costumes. And they make large amounts of money in return. But is that the role history should play in our world today? I think not. Although the films do deal with historical material, they are not always truly historical pieces of work. Very often, they are reflections of a culture but do not represent the thoughts and feelings of the people who lived then. They are almost like an escape from reality.

Historical films are not the only type of misconception of the discipline. Museums, historical sites, history texts and Internet sites all can serve as historical sources. But, in essence, they are sometimes more concerned with making money than revealing the true facts. Some films may try not to be a piece of the past at all and still turn out to be great contributions to people's understandings of how we once lived. Portrayals of daily life can be a resource to show how people in a certain place and time lived. As human beings, we can understand the positions these people were in. All we have to do is think about the factors affecting those people, and we will see history in the making, people reacting to what surrounds them. Almost as a primary source of study, it presents an objective view of the way we once were, adding to our understanding of how different our world has been from what it is today. One of the points is that in media, there is a motive for profit rather than genuine representations of the past, especially when there is a paying audience the work is targeting. Audiences targeted are often the young men and women who have plenty of interest in the popular films of today, which do not represent an interest in the past but in popular culture, as shown in movies and television, such as reality TV and music videos.

An often popularized application of historical thinking resides in the art of historical filmmaking. Before we can say anything, it is always important to consider that film production is a business run for the generation of money. Any film produced is for the purpose of creating revenue, whether through the incorporation of big stars to attract attention or huge budgets spent on special effects and costumes. These types of additions are always rewarded during the Oscars in an attempt to glorify the movie and generate more money. The simple concept is that they credit their own films for the self-aggrandizement and promotion of their own industry. Very often, this reflects the issues that affect the society in which we live the most. The war in the Middle East frequently raises awareness, ironically because the United States is at war there. These situations always attracts attention, as does any laws against violence toward minorities and the formation of the United Nations, which was designed to prevent the balance of power leaning too far to either side. So historical films have much relevance to us as a society because they not only remind us of past lessons learned but also show how they can be applied to our present situation, such as movies like the 1980s movie *Glory* about the struggle for black Americans to be soldiers in the Civil War, which still appears today with the struggle of blacks to be treated fairly by the police. These topics never change. They just appear in different contexts. After all, is there any difference between a parent who refuses to allow his or her son to be taught by a black teacher and one who refuses to sit in a section of the bus with a black woman in the 1960s? The simple fact that the issues never change is the same reason that historical movies are still important to our lives at the moment. Even though they may take place in the past, if they adapt to the changing circumstances, their point is still valid, making them another example of historical significance in our world now.

Another discipline that is often overlooked when we attempt to understand the historical value in a subject is theatre history. Often, when spectators decide to see a drama performance, they look through eyes that may or may not be educated. Very often, I assume the audience sees only the special effects, costumes and star actors, much like a film produced for the big screen. But theatre and any other type of performance have more to the show than the spectacle. There is an entire world behind what the audience sees at the performance. First of all, out of dedication to the craft, many plays are adaptations of the original, twisted and toyed with for a variety of reasons in order to produce something new and relevant. The main purpose is to relate to the world in which it is being performed. Dedication to the traditions of theatre's past shows in plays today. For example, Shakespeare has been repeatedly redone up to the present. The original plays were set in contemporary plays, he represents a black man or a negative American, both portrayed as savage years later. The important thing to remember is that the respect for tradition given to Shakespeare is a result of our society still dealing with issues that English society dealt with in the past. These familiar and reoccurring themes are a direct result of the simple fact that Canadians, Americans and many other Western cultures have our civilizations built upon the foundations created by the British. And so Shakespeare's commentary on the issues that he faced back in the seventeenth century is still relevant at the present time but in different forms, as in the Caliban example. Then one must conclude the importance of that historical tie to past cultures in order to understand ours currently. Recognizing mistakes made or successful political maneuvering could assist us in making better sense of how they failed or succeeded. Also the results of those actions in society in our present world make the knowledge of the past not only relevant to us today but a source of possible solutions to problems we encounter as humans.

Another aspect of our society to which historical thinking applies is the media. Even in advertisements, there are messages and a thought process hidden behind them. As advertisements target the audience of the time in which they are produced, they can also provide an excellent way to study cultures from the past. We can examine topics such as sexuality, politics, war and social trends, as to what the popular culture was indoctrinated with at that time. For example, if a passive viewer were to look at an advertisement from an early 1900s Sears catalogue showing a woman in a kitchen surrounded by new appliances, he or she would not see the historical content behind that photo. What an educated observer would see was that at that time, the woman's role was in the household, looking after her family. Not to mention, it would also be a reflection of the access to money that families had at a time when the economy was doing well. All of that could be taken from a dressed in a warm shirt and pants and sitting with his family by a fire in a lavish setting. Campaigning that his party believes in lower taxes on health care and incentives for people who work hard for their money, he was selling much more to the viewer than lower taxes for hardworking families. First of all, the scenery depicted already establishes that the conservative leader has enjoyed a measure of wealth. The fireplace and lavish scene appeal to those who feel the same way and most likely enjoy the same success, relating to them that he believes that the government should be run by people just like them. The inclusion of the family also targets those who have families, shown by the visual testimony that the conservative politician also has a family for whom he cares deeply. That appeals to family men all around the country who believe that if this candidate wins, he will take care of the country as well as his family or the country as a family, to go further. Of all the issues in an election, such as welfare levels, crime and foreign relations, the party proposed cuts to health-care taxes and an economy that supports hardworking families. Not only are those theoretical pillars for the conservative campaigns, but they directly affect wealthy, hardworking families. The simple atmosphere in which the family appears delivers the message that they need not worry about the cost of health care, as they have nothing to feel concerned about financially. The fact that he was sitting with his family in a comfortable warm sweater also strikes a soft spot. All of these aspects may not be apparent to the viewing eye. If, however, the observer has the ability to make those connections to past and present conservative platforms, he or she may have a better idea of what the party stands for. All of that thinking goes on simply because one has the ability to understand that there is more to what has been presented, a skill that historians learn when studying any piece of information. Whether a biography, a school textbook, a novel, a film, a presentation or an advertisement, all have a meaning deeper than just what appears on the surface. That would be one of the most important abilities historians provide for society and why history still needs to be part of the world we live in.

Historic Sites

ECENTLY, THE IMPORTANCE of history has at times shifted from the availability of books and resources to the concept of saving money. In my community, there is an old site, Montgomery's Inn, that represents a historical landmark in the formation of our community. Having withstood several cutbacks from the government, it has sought support from private, local historical organizations to survive. Is that the future direction that all sites must take to stay afloat? What is seen past the guided tours and the fancy setup is the significance the site has for the understanding of how our community evolved. Although the inn provides resources for school trips and local activities, like decorating the Christmas tree and offering farmers markets, these are done to keep the site operational by charging fees. What is most important is the preservation of a bit of our past. The house is decorated with pieces of furniture and art from the time that settlers moved to Toronto. But what many ignore is the life that it portrays. The presentation of the home of this wealthy innkeeper who owned most of the land we now live on would show how a successful Protestant landowner laid the foundations for this valuable property we all enjoy today. If a visitor were to walk through this inn, he or she would notice that the presentation of the rooms reflects that of someone who was very prosperous. But he or she would only recognize that interpretation if told, unless of course the visitor was looking for those aspects of the setup. The ability to direct one's attention to those factors would be from previous notification or insight provided from a guide. Otherwise, they would probably go unnoticed, and the success of the landowner would be overlooked. So the purpose of the tour could have been misunderstood or the point missed altogether.

With a historical background to the house, a spectator would then see that the innkeeper was wealthy, which enabled him to own such a large amount of land. It would also lead one to conclude what social status he held in the area, evident by his success and possessions. Since the inn was furnished with beautiful furniture and art, one must conclude that he did quite well for himself and was probably an influential member of the community. The point is that when a presentation of artifacts is given, a historian, educated in the history of the community, would question and inquire about the purpose of the articles and ask what could be learned from them, rather than simply seeing a chair for a chair. If a historical site is situated in a wealthy area, like the one discussed, then that site could be presented in a way that portrays a wealthy neighbourhood, with expensive furniture and structure. With a historical education, students would be able to identify the background of the presentation and come to a better understanding of the information incorporated in front of them. That theme of having the ability to understand more than simply the surface will be brought up many times throughout the book.

History and Museums

*A*NOTHER GOOD EXAMPLE of the presentation of artifacts is the displays at museums. Often, all of the exhibits are funded by organizations. And because of the financial concerns of many museums, they have to present what those organizations want to put on show. Even if it is not to make a profit, displays almost always have a particular purpose. For example, if an aboriginal showpiece is filled with artifacts collected from an aboriginal group, the museum will probably not want to show the artifacts in scenery that depicts today's poor reserve life. Rather, the organization would prefer to show them in a more favourable background. Here in Canada, our society sees aboriginals as an integral part of our history. However, some other countries, and even certain people here, perceive them as more of a savage people who should be portrayed as a problem, not as contributors to our society.

Museums and public historical sites are often products created by influences surrounding their existence if the funding is coming from an organization with a specific belief structure. Then those aims would be expected to reflect those interests.

The representation of historical information thus has an underlying theme, which can only be understood if the person is given that background information. The one problem with this type of communication from the historian to the passive viewer is that the point could be misunderstood. What the historian is trying to convey has perhaps been saturated with popular culture, leaving the message lost in the translation. The true story may fall victim to the need to give the viewer what he or she wants to see, what is pleasing to the mind. Therefore, the purpose of history in these representations may become remote and no longer important, bringing up the possibility that the display has lost some of its historical meaning and holds the reflection of what society desires, not what it should respect. That leaves the need for history as a tool for understanding all that is around us. And if the need or want for that type of knowledge disappears, so does the gift of historical understanding.

Education

The reason for the decrease in the desire for historians and their work could depend on the hard work and time it takes to become a historian. With the new wave of information available to the youth presently, research skills have shifted from reading books, following thoughts into the library and reading up on one's own interests. These are giving way to easy access to a massive amount of information, which only requires the student to Google a word rather than to look it up in a library. Their main driving forces are to generate more attention and thus wealth. Therefore, students who use the Internet have become consumers of information rather than evaluators of it. Instead of challenging their minds, the information presented to them is meant to please them, resulting in a situation where they want to be amused, not to use critical analysis of the meaning of the information. They take the path of least resistance, avoiding the more demanding but rewarding process of investigation meant to develop a work ethic and a discipline. The attitude developed then is that of how information is going to suit their needs rather than going out and researching data for the purpose of learning from it, making contributions to the issue and offering them for the common good.

One valid example of this type of research is that of finding more efficient ways of creating energy today. The intention of discovering a new energy source that is not harmful to the environment has been one of the most important and expensive ventures we as humans have had to take. Although the control and processing of that energy will be money-driven, the actual pursuit of it is meant to prevent environmental damage that affects us all. This is much like a history student who researches the causes of the war in the Middle East and our reaction to it in order for us to avoid the same disastrous result that terrorism has wreaked. With more work done on the past, we can learn from our mistakes and realize why people behave the way they do. Rather than not understanding both sides of the story or even the complex relationships that exist in cultures around the world, these can be brought to light by a firm grasp of history.

Theatre has been but one of many uses of historical thinking that has made a difference in how we see our world. As a student and teacher, I have always been presented with statistics when researching a topic. Most people would skip that page because of a lack of understanding of the relevance those numbers have to the topic. Very often, statistics could be considered a reliable source for proving political agendas, government success and failure rates on initiatives, business sales and population records of all kinds. The list goes on. But from a historian's point of view, those numbers tell more than simple data. Statistics, just like sources, can be used to suit certain needs. Most often, when indicators have been presented, they are misinterpreted. This could be an influencing factor that contributes to the reasons why those statistics show one picture but not the whole picture.

Primary Sources

Another attribute of the historian deals with the ability to look at primary sources, draw connections and come to conclusions based on the given evidence and prior historical knowledge. A primary resource, just to explain before I get started with the use of one, is a source or piece of evidence that has not been molested by any type of criticism or paradigm of thought to explain its existence. A fossil would be a good primary resource because its very existence has no constructed system or speculation attached to it. It is simply a fossil. If a historian or archeologist draws a theory from it, the theory would be considered a secondary source. Historians enjoy looking at primary sources because they intrigue them and they want to study them in greater depth. Remember what I was saying about how there are supporting factors behind an advertisement or other messages, more than just what you see? We look at primary sources in a way similar to that method of research but place the source in different contexts and relate its existence to the factors and forces that surround it. Once it has been proven that the source has direct connections to our knowledge of the past, we can then make an argument based on those findings. It is for sure that each professional could have different ideas and reasons for drawing conclusions from the primary source. But the source remains unbiased. People from various backgrounds approach primary sources for different motives, be they political or national, monetary or fame-related, religious, educational or territorial. Each theory about primary sources has its own motive for the conclusions stated, not to mention the judgment for approaching the source in the first place.

A good example of a primary resource was a record book of a church in my local area that I studied. Going into the assignment, I knew that I had to consider the fact that I was not just a university student writing a paper. Being nonreligious, I was also not familiar with the church. From simple notes recorded in the logbook, I was able to conclude that there was a very strong religious following, not of just one religion, but many. As a result of the successful integration of various religions and races, the church was used for a number of social gatherings and special occasions, ranging from picnics to wedding parties. Funds were collected and recorded for the purpose of church finances. After interviewing a long-time member of the community whose grandparents and great-grandparents lived there before and who was also interested in the logbook and the history of the district, I learned more. What seemed to have happened was that sometime in the 1960s, the government built public housing units, which changed the demographics of the area. The community, once surrounded by farms, transformed with the insertion of government expansion projects. For instance, paving for parking lots, new stores and crowded areas replaced a farming community that once thrived as a multicultural family. This created a division between those who owned the property and those who depended on the government for a place to live. That short history of a closely knit group of people was based on records at the town hall and an interview with a local resident. That is how a historian can take a primary source and trace it. What could be drawn from it provides a window into the past. But I knew from my background approaching this assignment, it could well have been viewed as otherwise.

A construction company could look at the installation of the buildings as a great profit, housing those who needed a place to live. Or a store manager could thrive from the business he or she received with the onslaught of new customers. There always has to be room for different perspectives, another reason for the historical discussion. In order to create an argument, you have to consider other points of view. This leads to a level of thinking that goes far beyond simple research and recitation, the discipline of historiography. Therefore, good historians depend on their knowledge of a subject extracted from years of research and experience, giving them the tools to examine sources and be able to put the information into context so the source has meaning in our world. Once a researcher comes to a conclusion about what he or she figures the source's meaning is, then other views can come into play, causing a discussion among like-minded people who bring their own backgrounds into play. The discovery of primary information often sparks this process between historians and drives them to examine things in the past as indicators of how we understand ourselves today.

When the topic of what it takes to be a historian comes up in discussion at gatherings, those who do not have a background in the subject often refer to it as a regurgitation of facts from the past. The point is to simply memorize important dates and figures and write them down in an essay or paper or answer a question on a test is not the true use of historical thinking. Neither is selecting the correct multiple-choice question for a mark or completing a fill in the blank for another mark. That does not make a good history student. That reputation is the reason why so many people lose interest in history. They ask themselves when selecting courses in high school how they can use this knowledge. Or at the university level, students will contemplate what they will do with a history degree. The subject has very few clear connections to a job or an occupation that will make them good money. Not to mention, most people find reciting facts and dates to be less exciting than, say, designing a website or learning how to build a bridge. The fact is that the attraction of the money made in those occupations also has an impact on the choice students make, especially when the job market in history has narrowed and seems to be having trouble keeping up with the wages of computer sciences and business jobs. The lure of history has been choked off in the younger generation, making universities academically based in the field have fewer students. But what they learn through years of studying history is that all that information provides the tools for a higher level of thinking. Having background knowledge for the part of history they are interested in at a higher level, historians often become experts in more specific areas. This allows the students to use that education to make connections to more complex issues. What would be the use of learning all that information and not seeing how it can be used? And once the connections have been made to wider discussions, then consideration of others' points of view will have an impact on the students' thinking. There is no arguing about what date the Civil War ended or the name of the first prime minister of Canada. Those facts are recorded and accepted as valid. But there can be discussions about some of the issues surrounding slavery and how they impacted the formation of the United States, and the problems Sir John A. Macdonald faced with confederation and how that shapes the country today can be debated. If a student does not even know what confederation is, then how will he or she be able to understand its impact on Canada's governmental structure, social fabric, minority arguments, aboriginal rights and so on when the time comes to look more closely at the topic? That is one of the main reasons that memorizing and reciting history to begin with is so important. There are ways to make it more interesting; that will be discussed later. Moving on to a higher level, or historiography, allows the student to become aware of more than just one simple argument. The mere skill of questioning sources would be a beginning when studying historical documents. Where do they come from? What is the date they were written? Who wrote them and from where? Were outside influences affecting the person's thinking? What is the context of when

History and Facts

*I*N PREVIOUS SECTIONS, I outlined some of the methods of how history as a discipline can be studied and the impact those may have on our world today. I would like to go further and discuss some of the practical purposes of history in the workplace. In my studies, I have come upon some fascinating uses of the study of history that extend beyond the boundaries of simple recitation of facts and dates. One such use would be building an argument based on sources, like primary, written, oral, videotaped, scientific and forensic, to prove a point. One excellent example of historical practice is that of detectives solving murders. They look at the evidence at the crime scene, question witnesses, use science to find clues left behind and construct an argument about what happened and who is guilty based on their findings. Without this skill and way of thinking, there would be no way to maintain justice, especially when there would be no reason for criminals to think twice before committing a crime or for people to refrain from breaking the law. Much like a professor writing a book based on the evidence he or she has come into contact with, how would we fully understand an argument without considering other points of view? Just imagine the control one would have if one was never questioned, especially in government, which has a huge amount of power over its people. The value of democracy is that we consider all sides when making decisions.

The practice of putting together a court case would be a good example of drawing a specific argument from sources. When a lawyer has been presented with a case to defend, he or she has to collect data about the client's story to prove that there is a chance that he or she is not guilty. In the case of a trial, all that the defense has to do is prove that there is a chance that the prosecution may not be 100 percent certain that the defendant is guilty. Historians approach a problem the same way. They wrestle with the facts and try to prove an argument, supported by evidence. Once the argument has been made, the opposing party—in a court case, that would be the defense—tries to question that proposal. What then happens is that the two sides end up presenting conflicting stories, either through the use of sources or witnesses. Using this information, the jury has to decide whether the defendant could be guilty without a doubt. Most important, for the purpose of this book, the argument created by the lawyers can be questioned. What results from that process is more of a discussion, searching for the truth, much like a trial with a jury. Or in the case of a historian, the academic community comes to their own conclusions. Therefore, court cases and the historiographical discipline have commonalities. Then from there, one can conclude the importance and evidence of its relevance in the practice of law. That may be why some companies look for people with historical research skills in order to research issues more effectively.

More recently, controversy has arisen about the relevance of archeological finds in the Middle East. The need for Muslims to gain access to their homeland requires not only military occupation but also a justifiable reason for why they should have ownership. The same goes for the Christians. What has been recorded in the Bible directly conflicts with the belief expressed in the Koran. Historians of each culture have their own reasons to claim the Holy Land. The Bible then traces back to historic occasions, like the exodus from Egypt and the destruction of the wall of Jericho. In order for them to prove their story of conquering Jerusalem, they have turned to evidence from the past to support their argument.

In that case, Christianity has turned to archeological finds in the area to prove that the stories in the Bible actually took place. And to do that, they looked to a scientist to uncover ruins to prove the legitimacy of the Bible. So many projects have recovered ruins of old fortresses that point to the fact that these events really happened. Although they have discovered ruins that may be directly related to the passages of the Bible, they still struggle with the complete absence of others. As these archeologists work away to prove that the basis for the religion actually exists, they are trying to win the argument that they have the right to occupy the Holy Land by using physical evidence. As I mentioned before, the discipline of history works the same way, drawing from this data or other sources for that matter, to construct an argument. It seems quite similar. What is more surprising is that some Muslims are researching information from the past, creating once again another side to the story or a conflicting point of view. The fact is that even when the issue is who has the right to the Holy Land, the use of historical research has great importance, rather than being just a discarded method of thinking.

History and Education

*A*NOTHER OCCUPATION THAT deserves some attention is the tedious job of the archivist, otherwise known as the librarian. From my experience dealing with the collection of materials, there is a lot more that goes into the job than a common person can see. While books have to be organized, simple alphabetical order does not suffice. Even libraries in middle schools have to be sorted into groups and headings. All of the materials in a unit of information must be similar in theme. Therefore, when a student or other interested person looks to the librarian for information on a topic, he or she knows exactly where to find it. Libraries do not exist just for the use of students but also for communities, societies and teachers themselves. Libraries also hold more than books. They can store materials such as magazines, films and newspapers, along with government documents. Libraries offer access to the Internet too. All of these items can be crucial to the understanding of past times. Some of these materials are often straight from the community; libraries serve as institutions that preserve the interests of the people who live there, very often having a collection of materials donated by local residents. The library then becomes a symbol of a neighbourhood, holding the history of those who live around it.

Communities are not the only people libraries serve. University libraries also have another purpose behind them. Higher education institutes specialize in certain subjects, such as law, medicine or military history. These collections must then focus on those subjects, narrowing down more general public libraries to specific themes. Therefore, when interested members seek out information for research on a particular subject, their resources are more concentrated in one place. Institutions for higher learning often are more specialized in topics than the high schools. The further up the educational ladder a student goes, the more complex the subject matter becomes. Not just that, but the material that is required reading becomes more remote and less useful and interesting to the rest of society. Consequently, many higher-level libraries are restricted to the certain few who need and want access to specific kinds of data. These are the people who must pay a fee for that particular material, like tuition at a college or university. This concealment of information in these libraries is what allows universities to make money. In order for a business to generate revenue, it has to have a desirable product. In the case of universities, unlike their little sisters and brothers in elementary and high schools that are publically funded, they are able to exist only if they are successful at generating large amounts of money to operate successful programs. This involves paying professors and teaching assistants and buying laboratory, classroom and office supplies, as well as covering property upkeep, administrator and office staff salaries and many other costs. Not only do they have the duty of concealing information from the public; they have to make their goods more desirable. In order to accomplish this, the universities offer degrees based on the knowledge they protect. And in order for that information to be available, a student has to pay a high price. The cost for this education has become increasingly higher because universities and their libraries are now faced with the information age of the Internet. An education could theoretically be obtained for free with the proper resources, a computer or public library, without the help of an institution for higher learning. So, in reaction to that threat, colleges and universities have claimed rights to the resources they have by blocking out those who do not have the money to pay them. After all, what would be the use of a degree from a private institution if you could achieve that diploma at no cost? Everyone would have a BA, rich or poor, free of charge, if there were no restrictions on the information provided in the schools. Metaphorically, the universities and colleges have built a wall between themselves and the general public, allowing only those with the highest average and most money to succeed. And the wall is growing higher as tuition rates increase. As marks become more important, the race for higher grades becomes more competitive. Now with the elimination in high school of the necessary preparation for future education, students are flooding the lecture halls with little or no knowledge of the work that is required to pass those courses.

Not only does the rise in cost for a postsecondary education make it more difficult for some to get into a program, but it also sends a lot of students into the working world where the money is just as good, if not better. A number of students graduating from university with degrees that have no practical use often find themselves faced with a dilemma. Find a job that pays well enough to survive or go back to school and get more qualifications. Both seem wrong. If a student spends all of his or her time and money on getting a degree, should there not be an occupation at the end of the road? Likewise, what is the purpose of an intelligent student who did well in studies working in a factory packing boxes or driving a truck? What seems to me to be the best solution is for a student to have a plan as to what he or she wants to do with a degree before earning it. Even though people very often change their minds during this process, they should set a goal. In the case of history, for the purpose of this argument, because the problem exists in all fields of study, the prospect of teaching is appealing to most. It is not just because their fathers or mothers taught but because it is a secure, challenging and rewarding job. We are always going to need teachers.

When I graduated from university, I was determined to go to teachers college. My marks became paramount to getting in. Not only that, but volunteer work and the proper selection of courses were required for admission. I ended up jumping through hoops of fire and having to take extra courses, including sign language, to satisfy the prerequisites for the teachers college I wanted to attend. But the important thing was to have a direction. As I have mentioned, the need for historians is great. Nevertheless, a student graduating from university has to understand that it takes more than just that degree to get settled into a career. Teaching history seems to be one of only a few of the practical purposes of studying history in the present-day workforce. Hence, there is a lack of enthusiasm in enrolling for history at the university level. This results in the program being underfunded, not receiving the money it needs to be as successful as it could be. But as I have argued, the importance of history in our society still exists. It just may appear in different ways. Above all, the research skills that one learns while studying the subject have a valuable part to play in our society. Should history then be available to all students, or should it be phased out as is being done right now? Does its importance have any impact on the economy? Does it play a role in the building of Canada as a nation? And if history is eliminated from the schools, how will people be introduced to it and become interested in learning about it if not in the classroom? These are all questions to consider when examining the discipline and its purpose in our society as Canadians and, furthermore, in the schools. It is the very fabric that defines who we are.

One of the biggest problems teachers face in the curriculum presently is the amount of material they have to convey to their students.

The broad spectrum of information needed to support the image of a Canadian is hard to cover. What seems to be happening is that the people who create the curriculum but do not have to teach it are distancing themselves from what is actually taking place in the classroom. This widening gap has put pressure on educators to teach what they can. The concept of a unified Canadian image has run into problems when there are so many histories that constitute the whole picture. Teaching children of the next generation is a big task if Canada is to be considered a combination of all of these cultures.

Supposing that Canada is to be unified under one flag, why do French Canadians have such an argument for their separatist cultural identity? And what about the aboriginals and Muslims who now make up a large part of our major cities? Furthermore, how are we going to educate them? Do they have to conform to a Canadian way of life, or are they allowed to practice their customs here in Canada? If history in the education system is meant to set the foundation of our future identity, the message is lost when the onus of the task is put on the teachers who cannot properly teach the content because of overwhelming demands on time and resources. Practically, not all the material can be covered, leaving many issues not addressed. The purpose of history in the classroom then becomes more of a prerequisite, which students have to pass, than learning the pride of their past. So when the importance of who we are becomes neglected, a fragmented country shows weakness as it becomes accustomed to personal gain rather than working for the good of all Canadians. While the appeal of financial gain, especially from the United States, benefits a few, it separates the rest of the nation from the advantages of economic growth. This separation creates cracks in the identities of all of us. Together, we stand. Divided, we fall.

History and National Identity

*I*n Canada, our identity is based on history teaching us who we are. The past explains what we are today. Take the aboriginal population as we see it at the present time, an example of our nation as a country with more than one culture and belief system. The question is whether there is a true identity. Quebec is another good example of how this country has differences in opinion on a unified nation. Even small towns spread all over our land each have their own definition of what Canada is. Do we see our home as a scattering of different cultures? This is a problem encountered in Toronto and other big cities, where people believe that Canada is based on immigration and the numerous advantages associated with multiculturalism. Investing in future immigrants will, we hope, mean that they are able to pass on their expertise to our population. Or should they conform to an established nation as they do in the United States? The problem becomes whether Canada's identity is based on a unified nation or a collection of people who define the state as a melting pot in which groups peacefully coexist with one another, each with its own idea of what the country should be. This is where history is important.

What we teach in our schools helps us understand what the future of our country will be. The underlying purpose of Canadian history is to give meaning to the state we as a country are in today. Tales told about the first contact immigrants had here and the building of the railroad across this vast land all lead one to conclude that the country was based on monumental achievements made by European and other settlers. And so the history of this country is based on these accomplishments, reinforcing the concept that Canada was built on the foundation of these European immigrants.

History then is a vehicle for promoting the unified nation under one umbrella. A country that is proud of its history promotes itself and encourages its people to believe that they owe a debt to the past settlers who created our identity. The vision of one happy group of co-operating citizens does present a complex problem here in Canada, mostly due to the deep-rooted cultures that exist beside one another. Unfortunately, these neighbours may not be friendly. The most studied of all are the French-speaking people of Quebec and their place within the rest of Canada. True, there are pockets of French people in other parts of the country as well who have their own set of demands, making the concept of a country with a common past difficult to justify. Even within the educational system in Quebec, not only is the language of instruction a controversial issue, but there exists a radically different understanding of how they evolved as a culture here in Canada. The history of Canada is based on polarizing events distinguishing them from English-speaking Canadians. These students see their past as one that is unique. This is different from what is taught in the rest of the school systems outside their borders. With an education system geared toward the promotion of having a separate past from the rest of the country, how is it possible to group them with other Canadian societies, each of which have their own set of beliefs, and teach that all Canadians have the same past? Do we take pride in a country where we are all happy side by side, coexisting with one another in an assortment of smaller groups? Or should we have a more centralized country in which everyone obeys the same laws and has the same understanding of our past, kept together by a cohesive government that cherishes the image of Canada as one nation? Through education, youth would learn that we are all brothers and sisters under the same flag.

The teaching of history in the school system has a big impact on how we, ourselves, and the rest of the world see and understand our country. Many factors come into play when we consider the role of history in our Canadian school curriculum. Most important, what does knowing our history do to strengthen us as a nation? Some may say that Canada is proud of its diverse heritage. Others may view the country as becoming more like the United States, unified all under one identity. So what role does history play in the formation of our past identity, especially as it is presently taught in the schools? The study of our past up to confederation is introduced at the elementary level. All of the students are exposed to that material. Knowledge of people and key events becomes crucial to the understanding of our heritage. But what is the purpose of teaching that information to the students? Is it to create a concept of Canada based on aboriginals and British and French relations or of European influence on our government? If the concept of a patchwork unified country works, why has it not been successful in other parts of the world, such as the United States? Canada has become dependent on the United States economically, specifically in the natural resources as well as commercial trade. Most of our entertainment comes from the United States. Our movies, our music, all hang in the balance of the United States. How is it possible for our country to avoid a cultural melting pot with our social mosaic when we depend so heavily on the American way of life? The incorporation of the aboriginals in the government through compensation for what they have been through is a good beginning. For Canada to recognize the aboriginal people who lived here long before European settlers arrived is a big step forward. In countries all over the world, the civilizations that inhabited the land before conquest have been exterminated or assimilated or are about to be treated that way. To recognize the religion, customs and way of life of aboriginals in Canada will contribute to the understanding of who we are.

Since our government structure is based on the British model, much like our legal system, the British still have a huge influence on our society. The concept of a British monarch ruling over our country has repercussions all the way down to the common person. While British beliefs in justice and religion have been imposed on everyone living here, the aboriginals are still having problems with the different cultures immigrating to this country. Is the British system of government necessarily the best way to govern a country of diverse people? For me, it comes down to the educational system—more specifically, the history part of it. If the point is to create a unified country with one belief where we all share the same past, why are there so many incongruences? In the school system, there are arguments about how we celebrate Christmas. The difficulties with prayer rooms and what a certain culture should wear to school increase tension. Hijabs and clothing, mercy killings, family abuse and food preferences all contribute to the problem of a united Canada. Dealing with these issues may lead to either more accommodations or less tolerance. Who's to tell which way the balance will go here in Canada?

My familiarity with the educational system starts in nursery school and continues on to a master of education degree. I have experience teaching in a multicultural school for a long while. What I learned in teacher's college was quite a contrast to how I have to teach in the classroom. Canada, the country in which I teach, has different purposes for education. Here, the driving force behind an education is to train students to become productive members of society, a society that includes and accepts all points of view. The problem then is what constitutes our idea of a country? In the United States, it seems that the curriculum, which is the one I studied when I went to teachers college in America, imposed a system of beliefs about their history that was predetermined. This historical foundation of the country was decided upon. Even the colleges are more concerned with making money by awarding high grades to those who attend to increase their reputation and thus attract more students and their money. Therefore, the driving force behind education, and history as a part of it, is to improve the economy. With the population as diverse and geographically spaced as it is, control overall is crucial for the purposes of generating wealth. With a segregated society, unrest, strikes, protests and crime, this could pose a serious problem to the efficiency of the economy. The role then that history has to play in keeping the country together under one common belief system really brings home the reason why history is taught in the schools.

In Canada, the purpose of history in the education system has another problem. As companies find more gain in the United States because of their higher profits, the social services, in particular the public education system, have to struggle to stay afloat. The big question then is which way will the education system turn—toward a unifying identity under one umbrella or one of moralistic representation? History therefore becomes the most important subject in the school. What is our identity? Do we turn to a more inclusive belief that we all share the same past? Or are we a creation of many cultures coming together? So when we teach history, should we concentrate on the events that brought us all together, World Wars I and II? Or do we focus on individual situations that occurred among people who have had a widespread impact on all of Canada? One of the difficulties with this approach is that the events may not have had an impact on all of us. What are we to teach then if no one is satisfied? Do students from one background share interest in one period and not another? How are we to accommodate all these different interests, not to mention the plethora of learning styles and varying needs? Historians who create the curriculum concentrate on what society needs most. But the educators are having difficulty teaching all this unfamiliar material because they are under a great deal of stress, having to learn all of the new course content that is required of them. Since the Canadian government supports a diverse country based on the past of our peoples and their varied experiences, the education system, which is meant to establish the foundation of such a country, expects too much from the teachers. And in the end, it is quite possible, due to time restraints, that not all of the material is covered. Failing to achieve this vision of a cultural mural of our past splits our youth because of neglect of some cultures and more attention on others. So the emphasis will depend on the preference of the teacher. The fact remains that not all cultures may be represented equally. Some will be more important in certain areas and some in others, depending on the geographical location, economic status and ethnicity of the area. In the end, that could cause interest in local histories and not national issues. This creates isolated pockets of knowledge about one's local histories but not that of a unified concept of Canada as a whole. It seems that the students have a choice as to whatever subject area they desire. While they may become experts on one topic, they do not understand how that fits into the big picture.

What Canada needs is a solution that suits all of us. And judging from the recent events here in Canada, aboriginal rights may be the glue that binds us together. First of all, aboriginal societies existed long before the Europeans arrived. The Europeans, the British in particular, imposed their beliefs on a people who were innocent to the ways of the Christian religion and its customs. And then with the human rights movement, which swept the world in the 1950s, natives were no longer the target for Christianization but victims of human rights violations. Harsh treatment by the Europeans of the aboriginals, as well as of other cultures who were minorities, soon became an issue. Although it is well known that not all tribes suffered the same affliction of mistreatment, it was universal among natives. It was not just in the schools; there was also systematic abuse by the Canadian government through reservation policies and the provision of care in those places. Even though the people were diverse, the cruelty was universal. Somehow, with a bit of luck, the regret for this poor treatment will unite Canadians. Piecing together all of these instances of abuse will, we hope, bring agreement and harmony, resulting in pulling the country together.

What remains, however, is a misunderstanding of the cruelty inflicted by our government on a people, furthering resentment on both sides. There are those who believe that history should protect our heritage and even create it or question it. Or in Shakespearean fashion, does the picture of the aboriginal represent the common Canadian view of minorities or outsiders from past to present? This image gives us a window into how Canadian society viewed natives and the rest of the world. Shakespeare commented on everyday lives in Elizabethan England. And that is represented in the images of the outsider, Caliban, and how they thought of the outsider or the exotic person. So too does the representation in the Ontario curriculum view native peoples and other European immigrants as those who are marginalized in our Canadian society. Just as the British government scrutinized those of an unknown origin, as in the original role of Caliban as a New World beast, the natives being viewed quite the same way reflects how the political and social structures view those who exist outside their own understanding of the world. What is most interesting is that today we

The Future

*T*HE FATE OF history lies in its importance. Since many movies and television programs are shifting to money making and the allure of the theatre and museums is fading, giving way to the sheer massive resource of the Internet, history has quite a challenge to overcome. The process of researching and questioning will always have importance in our society, or we are all doomed. The practice of it is waning in the school curriculum, but how we define ourselves as Canadians is now deeply rooted in our own cultures, not that of a unified society under one flag. History has to evolve if it wants to survive, much like an animal adapting to the changing climate. History may end up being remote when it comes to remembering the past, but we hope history can be useful in binding so many different stories together as one. We are making history as we speak and as we move into the future.

Printed in the United States
By Bookmasters